Jump! Jump! Jump!

Stacey

By Candelaria Norma Silva

Illustrations by Justin Aquidado

To request permission, contact the publisher at
author@candelarianormasilva.com.

Hardcover: 978-1-7351385-3-4
Paperback: 978-1-7351385-4-1
Ebook: 978-1-7351385-5-8

Library of Congress Number: 2021918312

First edition December 2021.

Cover design and illustrations by Justin Deocampo Aquidado

Published by Candelaria Norma Silva
Boston, Massachusetts USA

http://candelarianormasilva.com

THIS BOOK IS DEDICATED TO:

My children and my grandchildren:

Saige

Tommie

Amber

Cyrus

Everyone who's encouraged me, especially
my beloved husband, Tessil.

You, too
(Maddie, Unique, Darian, Dionna, and Leanne)

My Mom – Norma Jean Thompson

And 3 special people named Stacey:

Stacey Abrams who is an inspiring leader on behalf of Voting Rights in the United States and an author of fiction. (I imagine she had a vivid imagination and energy like the Stacey in this book.)

Stacy C., a beloved new member of our family.

Stacy S., my long-lost friend. I miss you and hope that you are well.

"Okay, Ladybug," Mom says.

"Go out and run off some of that energy. I'll call you when it's time for your nap."

I'm going to jump, jump, JUMP.

I'm going to jump, jump, JUMP!

On and off the tree stump.

"How's it going, Stacey?"

Mom calls from the back door.

"It's not time for

my nap yet, is it?"

"Not yet. I was just

checking on you."

I'm going to hop, hop, HOP.

I'm going to hop, hop, HOP!

Until I decide to stop.

"Ten-minute warning, baby-girl,"

Mom says.

Nooooooo!

"I don't WANT to

take a nap!"

"You've got a little

more time... relax."

I want to skip, skip, SKIP.

I want to skip, skip, SKIP!

I might even do a flip.

"Naptime, Stacey,

come in NOW!"

"I. Don't. Want. To.

Take. A. Nap!"

♪ "Take that bass out your voice,

Miss-missy," Mom sings. ♪

I need to dance, dance, DANCE.

I need to dance, dance, DANCE!

"Please, Mama,

give me another chance."

"If I have to call you one more time little girl, I'm coming to get you," Mom yells.

"It's no fair! I'm not even sleepy..."

I don't want to take a nap.

I start to twirl, twirl, TWIRL.

I start to twirl, twirl, TWIRL!

All around my backyard world.

"I'm going to count to ten, Stacey.

One, two, three, four...

Ready or not, you must come in."

I want to shake, shake, SHAKE.

I want to shake, shake, SHAKE!

I like the sound my beads make.

I hear the back door squeak.

Oh-oh, she's really coming now.

"Mama, please,
can I just sit on the
porch and read?"

I think I'll sit, sit, SIT.

I think I'll sit, sit, SIT!

For just a little bit.

"Give me your hand.

You don't have to go to sleep,

but you must lie down."

"I *(yawn)*

don't *(yawn)*

want *(yawn)*

to take *(yawn)*

a nap."

"Can I sit on your lap, Mama?"

"No, you cannot. Now get

your hiney to your room!"

I think I'll crawl, crawl, crawl.

I think I'll crawl, crawl, crawl!

My legs feel a little tired, that's all.

I'm on the bed, bed, bed.

I'm on the bed, bed, bed.

I'm just going to rest my head.

ZZZ

PURRRR...

zzzZZ

I fall asleep, sleep, sleep.

I fall asleep, sleep, sleep.

Don't let me sleep too deep.

ABOUT THE AUTHOR

Candelaria Norma Silva's writing is inspired by her childhood in a large extended family in St. Louis, Missouri. She remembers learning to read in first grade. Soon becoming an insatiable reader, young Candelaria checked out as many books as possible from the library each week. She still loves to read, with special affection for reading and collecting children's books that feature children of color.

Writing is one of the ways Candelaria celebrates family and community, and shares stories that reflect her experiences as a child, sister, mother, grandmother, friend, and citizen.

Candelaria lives in the Dorchester community of Boston, Massachusetts, with her husband. She looks forward to long summer "take-over" visits from her grandchildren. *Jump! Jump! Jump! Stacey* is her second book featuring Stacey. Her first book, *Stacey Became a Frog One Day*, was published in October 2020.

ABOUT THE ARTIST

Born into a family of artists in 1993 in the countryside of Iloilo, Philippines, Justin Deocampo Aquidado has been drawing for as long as he can remember.

Young Justin had a competitive spirit. He competed in multiple contests during his elementary and high school years where victories became his achievements and losses became his lessons. As a child, he dreamed of becoming a well-known comic illustrator.

College was a busy time. Justin pursued a Bachelor of Science in Architecture, graduating in 2015. During his last two summers of college, he worked as a summer art teacher for children. After graduating, he worked as an architect, while also becoming an illustrator, his true passion.

Justin plays guitar and video games avidly. He is also a collector of action figures and assembles model kits. *Jump! Jump! Jump! Stacey* is his second collaboration with Candelaria Norma Silva.

WITH GRATITUDE

What a tremendous community of friends, family members, acquaintances, colleagues, and people I have yet to meet the Stacey books have engendered. I am deeply grateful to everyone who purchased my first book, *Stacey Became a Frog One Day,* and to those who purchase this book.

Jump! Jump! Jump! Stacey could not have happened without the diligence of Paula Ribeiro, who acted as project manager and graphic designer. I tracked you down 20 or so years ago when I saw a brochure you designed that I absolutely loved. Working with you on various projects has been delightful.

I must acknowledge Delanda Coleman, the angel who came into my life in early 2020 and helped me get *Stacey Became a Frog One Day* into print. Delanda's books, *More Than A Princess* and *What's My Superpower?* should be on every young child's shelves. (Available on SydneyColeman.com)

For a signed copy of *Jump! Jump! Jump! Stacey,* order at: candelarianormasilva.com

Stacey Became a Frog One Day

With imagination, Stacey can be anything! Stacey Became a Frog One Day, and each day of the week she has fun as a different animal. When will she be a kid again? Join Stacey's reverie in rollicking rhyme and rhythm to find out.

Stacey Became a Frog One Day and
Jump! Jump! Jump! Stacey are available from:

candelarianormasilva.com
Amazon.com
IngramSpark.com

Contact the author:
author@candelariasilva.com

Also, check your local bookstore!

CPSIA information can be obtained
at www.ICGtesting.com
Printed in the USA
LVHW070828230223
739874LV00034B/865

9 781735 138534